FAIRIES

CELEBRATIONS FROM SEASON to SEASON

A FAIRY BOX BOOK

ADRIENNE KEITH

ILLUSTRATED BY WENDY WALLIN MALINOW

A SWANS ISLAND BOOK

TRICYCLE PRESS
Berkeley, California

TRICYCLE PRESS
P.O. BOX 7123
Berkeley, California 94707

Book and cover design by Wendy Wallin Malinow
Library of Congress Cataloging-in-Publication Data
Keith, Adrienne
      Celebration fairies: from season to season: a fairy box book / Adrienne Keith; illustrated by Wendy Wallin Malinow.
          p. cm.
      "A swans Island book."
      ISBN 1-883672-23-6
      1. Children's poetry, American. 2. Seasons—Juvenile poetry. 3. Fairy poetry, American. I. Malinow, Wendy Wallin, ill. II. Title.
PS3561. E37577C45 1995
811'.54—dc20   94-42366
                                                                CIP
                                                                AC
First Tricycle Press printing, 1995
Manufactured in Singapore 1 2 3 4 5 6 7 8 – 00 99 98 97 96 95

To my mother—with thanks for my first goody box, and for so many little treasures; and to my father—with love from his Bunny Girl.—A.K.

To Louise for a lifetime of support and to Seba, Max, and Chester for my daily inspiration.—W.W.M.

In every single season
fairies always find a reason
to celebrate the simple things
like ice and rain and sunlit wings.
Through festivals and fairy food
they revel in each season's mood

and savor all the scents and flavors
with gifts and games and feasts and favors.
So be a little fairy, too,
and celebrate the way they do —
come see the world through fairy eyes
where life is full of sweet surprise.

Here's a list of what's in store
inside this book of fairy lore:

Festivals
Feasts — to set the mood
with tasty fairy food

Favors — for Nature's friends in need
(thoughtful ways to help and feed)

Games — to play, just for fun
Special Gifts — to give someone

when fairies meet in friendly groups
to sip hot cider, tea, and soups
and leap in heaps of leaves for fun
because the fall has just begun.

FALL

FAVOR

Sunflower Snack

Dried sunflowers always please hungry birds up in the trees.

Hang a seed head from a string— soon the birds will come and sing.

FALL

GAME

CIRCLE CHANT

Like leaves swirling to the ground,
hold hands tight and whirl around.
Turn a circle seven times
while chanting favorite fairy rhymes.

"Whenever loving fairies meet, their eyelash kisses are so sweet."

"Whenever fairy neighbors meet, they shake each other's hands and feet."

"Fairies always hug good-bye as they're taking off to fly."

GIFT

ROSEHIP TOPS

Red rosehip tops really spin
(be sure a bit of stem's left in).

Present one in a walnut shell
and show friends how to spin it well.

FALL

FESTIVAL
Skating Social

When ponds and puddles freeze clear through
and all the world's an icy blue,

fairies ski until quite late
then take a peaceful moonlit skate,

or cuddle up in hollow trees
away from winter's chilly breeze.

WINTER

FEAST

MAPLE SNOW

Drizzle maple syrup twice
on fresh snow or scoops of ice.
Don't be dainty — that's the worst—
fairies eat this treat face first!

FAVOR

PINE CONE PIE

This recipe for pine-cone pie
will serve three critters who drop by.
Mix a mud dough, top with cones,
serve with nuts on pie plate stones.

WINTER

SNOW FAIRIES

Fairies lie back in the snow
and flap their arms till snow wings show,
then jump right up and turn around
to see a fairy on the ground.

SPRING

FESTIVAL

PLANTING PARADE

To the garden go the fairies
dressed as daisies, peas, and cherries.

FESTIVAL

They wear strands of bright dew beads
and carry baskets full of seeds,
to plant flowers that smell sweet
and luscious food for all to eat.

SPRING

Tea Time

When pouring for a fairy friend,
smiles are proper, pinkies bend.
Offer cakes and mint-leaf tea.
"Please" and "thank you" are the key.

FAVOR

ANTPASTO

A picnic isn't really through until the ants have eaten, too. So crumble up a bit of bread to be sure that they're well fed.

SPRING

Hide and Seed

Run and hide and plant five seeds
(watch for seekers in the weeds).

Hurry quickly back to base —
the one who's caught has to chase!

1 2 3 4 5

GIFT

Petal Posies

Tuck posies with rosy faces into secret hiding places to cheer a friend on their way home from school or out to play.

SPRING

FESTIVAL
GARDEN GATHERING

In floppy hats and flowered shirts,
with parasols and petal skirts,
fairies play croquet and cricket
then snooze awhile in the thicket.

And as the summer sun sets low,
they dance together in its glow.

SUMMER

FEAST

Blueberry Cream

A perfect summer treat for fairies:
ice-cold milk on fresh blueberries.

To make it even more supreme,
add a dollop of whipped cream.

FAVOR
WATER SOUP

When gardens start to wilt and droop,
mix up a cup of water soup.

Bloom!
Flourish!
Thrive!
Grow!
Grow! Bloom!
Grow!

Before the flowers drink it up,
add good wishes to the cup.

SUMMER

GAME

MOONLIGHT, SUNLIGHT

This is a game of stop and go.
When "sunlight" is called, run on tip-toe.
Race straight ahead—the end is in sight—
but stop if a fairy calls "moonlight."

GIFT

FLOWER DOLL

A pansy face always charms,
twigs work well for legs and arms.
Tie it all with grassy thread.
Deliver in a blossom bed.

SUMMER

A handy little carrying case,
this **FAIRY BOX** is just the place
to keep the goodies that you find—
treasures of the fairy kind.

So take along your **FAIRY BOX**
when you step out on daily walks.

Fill it up with stones and shells,
wishes, seeds, and flower bells
to use for fairy celebrations
and all the seasons' jubilations.

✸ ✸ ✸